D0382743

This Book Belongs to:

Friends
of the
Danville Library

This item is a gift
from the

Friends of the Danville Library

Perfectly Percy

story and pictures by Paul Schmid

HARPER

An Imprint of HarperCollinsPublishers

This is Percy.

Percy is a porcupine.

The thing that makes Percy

the very happiest is . . .

BALLOONS!

Red balloons.

Blue balloons.

Round balloons.

Curly balloons.

But HAPPY little porcupines
with balloons are soon
SAD little porcupines.

The balloons always go POP!
And Percy's happiness pops with them.

What's a little porcupine to do?
Percy did not want to cry.
Percy did not want to give up.

Percy thought he must think.

Percy sat.

He closed his eyes tight.

But no thoughts came.

Well, useful thoughts, anyway.

Percy decided he needed
some help.
He asked his big sister, Pearl.
She was smart.

But her ideas were not
very practical.

Percy went to ask his mom,
but she was too busy to help much.

Percy thought it was time
to go back to thinking
for himself.

He thought things
all the day.

He thought thoughts
through the night.

By breakfast time
Percy thought he was
out of thoughts.

But then . . .

Percy had an
IDEA!

A BIG idea.

A marvelous idea.

A perfectly Percy idea.

Have fun, Percy!

For Linda, who makes me
the very happiest

Perfectly Percy
Copyright © 2013 by Paul Schmid
All rights reserved. Manufactured in China.
No part of this book may be used or reproduced in any manner whatsoever without
written permission except in the case of brief quotations embodied in critical articles
and reviews. For information address HarperCollins Children's Books, a division of
HarperCollins Publishers, 10 East 53rd Street, New York, NY 10022.
www.harpercollinschildrens.com

Library of Congress Cataloging-in-Publication Data
Schmid, Paul.
    Perfectly Percy / by Paul Schmid.
        p.   cm.
    Summary: Percy the porcupine loves balloons but he must find a way to keep them
from popping.
    ISBN 978-0-06-180436-6 (trade bdg.) — ISBN 978-0-06-180437-3 (lib. bdg.)
    [i. Balloons—Fiction.   2. Porcupines—Fiction.]   I. Title.
PZ7.S3492Pe   2013   2011030447
[E]—dc23   CIP
                                                                              AC

The artist used pencil on paper and Adobe Photoshop to create the illustrations for this book.
Typography by Dana Fritts
13 14 15 16 17   SCP   10 9 8 7 6 5 4 3 2 1 ❖ First Edition

3190105184 7863
WITHDRAWN